I0682424

THE UNWITTING ASSASSIN

ASSASSIN

The Murder of JFK

A Novel by Rick D. Cleland

Order this book online at www.trafford.com
or email orders@trafford.com

Most Trafford titles are also available at major online book retailers.

© Copyright 2010 Rick D. Cleland.
All rights reserved. No part of this publication may be reproduced, stored
in a retrieval system, or transmitted, in any form or by any means, electronic,
mechanical, photocopying, recording, or otherwise, without
the written prior permission of the author.

Printed in Victoria, BC, Canada.

ISBN: 978-1-4269-2858-1

*Our mission is to efficiently provide the world's finest, most comprehensive
book publishing service, enabling every author to experience success.
To find out how to publish your book, your way, and have it available
worldwide, visit us online at www.trafford.com*

Trafford rev. 3/1/2010

www.trafford.com

North America & international
toll-free: 1 888 232 4444 (USA & Canada)
phone: 250 383 6864 ♦ fax: 812 355 4082

CHAPTER ONE

What to do about Jimmy Hoffa
– he knows too much about us

Jimmy Hoffa had been accused of a lot of things by the Federal Government. It covered the entire gamut of illegal activities. He was President of the International Brotherhood of Teamsters and he and they controlled the trucking industry Nationwide. He had used the members' Union dues and their contributions into its Retirement Fund at will. Some of its members were known to have intimidated those who would not bow to Hoffa's demands of them. Some of Hoffa's methods were subtle, others overt and quite vivid. The more overt and vivid involved limbs broken with baseball bats, others, more subtle, involved bricks thrown through living room windows while the residents were peacefully watching TV in the room, and family members briefly kidnapped. The tacit message was always the same – "go with the program, do as you're told, don't step out of line and tell noone what you're told to do, not even your wife, OR ELSE. If there is a next time, the brick will be a Molotov Cocktail and we'll burn down your entire house, including anyone inside, capisce?" That was the way the Teamsters did business with the reluctant or the uncooperative, pure and simple.

Jimmy Hoffa had come up through the ranks of the Trucking business and was, perhaps its earliest proponent and Organizer for the "outward purpose" of Collective Bargaining with those whose products needed trucks to move from point of manufacture, to point of sale. The "public side" of James Riddle Hoffa was that of an ardent supporter of Studs Terkel's working stiff. He was constantly working to improve the wages and working conditions for those who drove trucks for a living. Then there was the "other side" of Jimmy Hoffa. That was the ruthless, obsessed man who craved power and, along with it, the ability to cripple the transportation system of the entire Nation, almost at will. Early-on, Jimmy Hoffa had decided to curry "associates" within the Underworld, whose Dons and Capos he would reluctantly need because their hands had long fingers into the darker side of Organized labor across the entire United States. Hoffa would roam the docks where trucks loaded and unloaded. He would, on occasion, climb into a trucker's cab and ride with him for part of a day in order to gain the driver's confidence for an "aye" vote when it came time for a vote to be taken on whether a given "shop" would allow its workers to Unionize. Any driver or dock worker who gave Hoffa's overtures the cold shoulder, would be somehow "summarily" dealt with by a word or two to the Enforcers within the "Mob". Jimmy Hoffa would later become key to unraveling the plot to kill the young President in a most bizarre sort of way.

CHAPTER TWO

The Would-be Detective

Matthew (Matt) Clemmons was a self-described "two-bit gumshoe" and political "junkie". He had grown up in suburban Westchester County, just north of the Bronx and attended Mamaroneck High School in the late 1950s. Nothing in High School had particularly either kindled or sparked his academic interest, and so he managed to "limp" to graduation. One thing, however, did interest him. Unfortunately, there was no Subject in High School that was devoted to that particular Subject – it was Politics. He was drawn to the remarkable success of Dwight

David Eisenhower, as an Army General whose tactics and strategies had defeated Fuhrer Adolph Hitler and the German Third Reich in Europe. "Ike", as Eisenhower was widely known, returned to the United States victorious and was courted to run for the Presidency by both the Democratic and Republican parties. Yes, Ike was most interested in making the run for the White House. Initially, the General was drawn to the Democratic Party. There was, however, one very big problem with that. There was already someone else interested in running for President as a Democrat. That was Senator Adlai Stevenson of Illinois. Even with the huge popular support which Ike enjoyed as a result of his victory in Europe, Adlai Stevenson could be a formidable opponent in a Primary Election which Ike's desire and ambition would force. Ike was most reluctant to have win another victory so soon, especially one in the Political Arena, Therefore, Eisenhower took the path of least resistance, ran as a Republican and was Elected President. During the Campaign, Ike was in a motorcade which wended it way North, from New York City, along US 1 (also known as the Boston Post Road) all the way to Boston. Matt Clemmons was standing on the sidewalk as the motorcade passed through Mamaroneck, then through Rye, Harrison, Port Chester and onward into Connecticut.

At about the same time, there was a young and charismatic Democratic Senator from Hyannis Port, Massachusetts. He was from a very political family headed by Banker Joe Kennedy who was married to Rose Fitzgerald.. Joe's oldest son, Joseph was being groomed for the US Presidency until he was killed in the Pacific during World War II. With the younger Joseph no longer available, the Family Patriarch turned his attention to son #2, John Fitzgerald Kennedy.

Matt's interest in Politics was, by now, very keen. However, he was too young to do much more than read about it and study it as he did when he went to College and Majored in Political Science. He was becoming consumed by politics, to the detriment of the many other Courses he was forced to take also. In a Liberal Arts curriculum, such as Art and Music Appreciation paled by comparison with such as Historian Theodore White's ongoing series of books, "The Making of the President ......" and William Manchester's "Douglas Mac Arthur, American Caesar". He just could not find the interest necessary to study and try to identify with the French, Dutch, and Flemish Masters of Landscapes and Still-life Portraits. Thus, his mastery of Political Science was dragged-down, grade-wise, by the subjects in which he had little or no interest. He finally did graduate with a notably lackluster overall academic performance.

He had become fascinated by the televised (in black and white screen only) Congressional hearings held by "HUAC" (House Unamerican Activities Committee), Chaired by Senator Joseph McCarthy of Wisconsin. McCarthy had managed to ruin many a life by simple, accusation, rumor, inuendo, insinuation, that a Witness appearing (mostly by subpoena) before his Committee either had been or was a Member of the Communist Party of America.. Joe McCarthy's finger pointed at a person testifying, was tantamount to a summary verdict of Guilty. Matt wondered, in awe, how such a person could accumulate such unbridled, unrestrained power as just one Member of a body in which every State had to Members? Where were the checks and balances? Where were the voices which were surely opposed to such tactics and actions? Had they all left their brains and consciences outside when they entered the Senate Chamber? Matt had been a very young lad during the time of the televised HUAC McCarthy Hearings. Yet they made quite an impression on him. Senator McCarthy had done, verbally, what the Mafia had been doing literally

– destroying those who didn't see things their way and instantly "fall in line". After graduation from College, Matt had taken a job which both give him a paycheck and allowed him "first hand" experience in the broader arena of Politics. He became an Apprentice Newspaper Reporter in New York City. He would quickly learn, much to his dismay, that there were certain events which you might witness, but dared not report on, unless you wanted to try to be Harry Houdini, trying to escape from ankle chains in about 40 feet of water somewhere around Manhattan Island. Houdini might have been able to do it, but not with a bullet between his eyes. Matt had been sitting around the Office with not much going on, when he decided to splurge for lunch. He went to "Danny's Hideaway" Restaurant, in Manhattan, owned by Danny Stradella. It was a known lunchtime hangout of the Who's Who in the News and Entertainment Business. Often seen there were such as Walter Cronkite, Erik Sevareid, Lucille Ball, Walter Winchell, Art Buchwald. He might even run across TV Reporter Bernard Shaw and get some good leads for later in the day or week. Seeing no sign of any Celebrities and no sign of Bernie Shaw, either, Matt decided to take a leisurely stroll back to his Office, since it was a beautiful, sunny day. He had walked several long blocks when he came upon a black limo that was double-parked in a "No Standing" zone. Hmmm, thought Matt, must be the Major or some other dignitary. Might be somebody from the UN Building, but the limo did not have Diplomatic tags. The limo happened to be partially blocking a parked car from getting out into the road. The driver got out and rapped on the rear deck of the limo to get the driver's attention. Out came the driver in full limo-driver uniform, complete with a black, short-brimmed hat. The two men exchanged some works and tempers quickly flared. THAT'S when Matt saw it all and wished he hadn't seen any of it. The limo driver popped open the trunk lid of the black car. He then reached inside his black jacket, pulled out a pistol with a silencer, stuck it into the stomach of the other man and pulled the trigger twice. Matt heard only two "hisses" as the bullets found their deadly mark. Before the blood could flow, the victim had doubled-over the right thigh of the driver, who then, with an upward thrust of his entire right leg, tossed the dead man's body into the trunk of the limo, shut the lid, and returned to he place behind the wheel of the limo. Almost immediately, an extremely neatly dressed man, wearing his overcoat (which he really did not need in the balmy weather) only over his shoulders, ducked into the rear right seat of the limo which immediately drove away. Matt was stunned, speechless. The entire incident had taken less than a minute, total. Matt had seen a Mafia killing, yet he knew, for all practical purposes, he had seen nothing at all. That's what could happen if you argued with the wrong person, at the wrong place and time. The whole incident had been surreal, so non-chalant, so unemotional, so like how the Mob operates. Matt could only just shake his head as if he had just been shaken, in the bed, from a bad dream. Matt finished his walk back to his Office, wrapped up some paperwork and thought he'd stop off at a bar before catching the Subway to his apartment in Brooklyn. Then he cancelled the idea. The booze might get him into a talkative mood and he might say too much and get his ass in trouble "big time". Best to try to convince himself that what he KNEW he had seen, was just some sort of a mirage. He really hadn't seen a man killed for no reason other than yelling at the wrong person at the wrong time and place. He forced himself to just "blank the whole thing out of his mind" as if it had never REALLY happened at all. Yeah, Matt, that's it. Forget the whole damned thing – it nevvah 'appened at all, period, he said to himself and forced himself to accept that and go home and get some rest and get ready for tomorrow.

It wasn't long thereafter, that Matt was at a party of a friend of his from College on Long Island. The party was really in the basement of a three-story brownstone "walk-up", meaning that the house had no front yard, per se. There was a keg of beer in the basement, and several young people had gathered around it and were chatting. Matt's friend came downstairs and "invited" all of them to move upstairs for just a few minutes. Matt was the last to do so. The request seemed rather odd to Matt. Maybe the keg had run out and they were going to deliver the fresh keg through the iron doors which, on a brownstone walk-up, typically lay flat on the outside and must be raised and propped open, leading the way to the stairs to the basement. This would be similar to the doors leading to a mid-western tornado shelter of concrete, sunk in the ground in the backyard of a house. Matt delayed his "exit" from the basement just long enough to see two men emerge from some other entrance into the basement, carrying something large and wrapped in a sheet over their shoulders. Whatever it was, they dropped in on a large area rug on the floor. Then they rolled up the rug, tossed it back over their shoulders and carried it up the stairs, through the opened iron doors to the front and placed it into the trunk of a waiting car. Matt knew, immediately, there had been a Mafia "elimination" somewhere nearby and this is how they were getting rid of the dead body. It was just another example of what Matt had known for some time. You don't mess with the Mob. They kill at will, swiftly, precisely and deftly. There are neither witnesses nor funerals. Since the Mafia is almost exclusively Roman Catholic, rarely, but occasionally, one who has killed with some sense of remorse, will confess to a Priest, on his deathbed, so that his conscience will be clear as he enters the life hereafter. The Priest must then decide, morally and ethically, whether any harm can be done to anyone still living, by the disclosure of the confession he has heard, and act accordingly. Most often, what has been disclosed to a Priest in the Confessional, stays there, eternally.

Matt had now, on two separate occasions, witnessed how the Mob did business. He wondered if there was a way to "think like they did", not to prevent what they had planned on doing, put to be able to "piece it together" after the fact. If one were to be able to do so, one could either verify History, or re-write History as it actually happened. Matt had a gut feeling that much of Political History had to be re-written in light of unearthed facts. History just, simply, could not be let to stand as the WARREN COMMISSION had determined it to be. Matt was certain of that. Would it be Matt's destiny, in Political History, to seek, find, and report the facts as they really were. Would it be solely up to Matt to somehow expose the workings and findings of the Warren Commission to be the total fraud that his gut told him they were? Matt had challenged himself. Now, he had no choice but to live up to his own challenge. He must pursue, doggedly pursue, until he had satisfied himself (screw the naysayers) that yes, the Warren Commission was a fraud. However, more importantly, we, over forty years later, still do not know who REALLY President John F. Kennedy. Matthew Clemmons would find the answer and the Nation could finally call Kennedy's Assassination, "CASE CLOSED". It would become Matt's obsession, but he must guard against "easy answers" and anyone too eager to confess for whatever reason. Nobody would "rewrite" the murder of JFK simply to preempt the unknown Political "junkie", Matthew Clemmons, from doing so. Matt didn't give a damned about who could claim the credit for solving the mystery (and mystery is still was).

He only gave a damned about causing the truth to come out, FINALLY. The truth had to come out. It just had to. It obsessed Matt. It, at times, possessed him. Matthew Clemmons would get to the bottom of who actually killed President Kennedy if it took his last living breath to do so. To Matt, it was just that simple.

Now, Matt would have to travel to Dallas, Texas. He would find out what he could there and then work his way back to wherever the trail would lead. He had a gut feeling that the name Hoffa would crop up again. If it did, he would follow that trail to wherever it might lead, with absolutely no preconceptions to maybe lead him astray. Matthew Clemmons was determined.

CHAPTER THREE

Studying the Scene of the Crime

Matthew Clemmons, obsessed as he was with how it could have happened, boarded a flight from New York's La Guardia Airport for the flight to Dallas/Fort Worth Airport. He had been unable to book a flight directly into Dallas' Love Field, where the former President had flown into on the short flight from Fort Worth's Carswell Air Force Base. The Air force Base had been basically shut down due to Congressman Dick Armey's Base Closure Act, intended to reduce both waste and duplication of services provided by the Department of Defense. Dyess

Air Force Base to the West of Fort Worth would remain open. Dallas Naval Air Station in south Dallas had suffered the same fate as had Carswell Air Force Base. Therefore, Matt Clemmons flew into D/FW Airport and took a taxi from there to downtown Dallas. He considered, briefly, visiting the nightclub owned by Jack Ruby who had shot Lee Oswald, but decided that such a side trip did not fit into his itinerary for fact-finding, at least not on this particular occasion. Matt was more interested in the route the Presidential motorcade had taken from Love Field to where the shots, fatal to the young President had allegedly then fired. Matt wanted to retrace the last mile or so of that route, almost literally, foot-by-foot. He was convinced that somewhere in that last mile lay either the clue or the answer to who killed the President. The answer had to be there. There was nowhere else it could be. The possibilities as to how the shooting occurred were finite. Any competent investigator could narrow down the entire fatal scenario to one City block. That City block could be reduced to square yards to square feet. Anything that moved or existed within that given area, well, someone had to be seen, from squirrels to birds (pigeons), to children idly playing, to whatever, it had to be smelled, heard, whatever, by someone other than Emile Zapruder whose camera had shot what were presumed to be the work of the assassin of JFK. Yes or no? Matt was not convinced, either way. Dan Rather once said, "the Camera Never Blinks" and wrote a book to support that finding. Well, the camera may never blink, but the film contained therein can be altered as evidenced to support a desired outcome of an event. Matt was going to walk the last five hundred or so yards driven by the Presidential limo prior to the fatal shooting. He got out of the cab a couple of blocks short of Dallas' Dealey Plaza and started walking. He would walk the same route as had the Presidential Limo. He turned right, walking toward the Texas Schoolbook Depository Building and back to the left alongside that building. He stopped right about the spot where the shots hit the President and looked back and up toward the window from where the gunman had fired. Damn, it was an absolutely clear shot. He wondered why the Secret Service had not secured that building before the Motorcade? Was it a mere oversight? Did they even bother to do those kinds of things back in 1963? Maybe they thought that the President was so close to the cover and safety of the railroad overpass that did not occur to them to cover THAT possibility. To his right front, Matt could see the embankment leading up to the "grassy knoll". A gunman would have had a clear and perfect shot from there. One thing bothered Matt and would keep coming up in his thought process. He was now into the mental "territory" of supposing. What if the killing was a carefully prepared Mob "hit"? Hitmen are professionals. They fire one fatal shot and then pack up and leave the scene. They go by the Sniper's Motto of "one bullet, one shot, one kill". Any other method would be regarded as "messy" and highly unprofessional. The local police and even the Secret Service would be looking for a semi-automatic rifle with a handful of spent cartridges left at the scene of the firing of the weapon. Nobody would be looking for a one-shot weapon, in particular. Not in 1963 the would not have been. So, that leaves this nutso guy, unknown to almost everybody, who goes off one his own and gets in a couple of deadly shots just before the paid assassin has a chance to shoot. Instant havoc and mayhem breaks out all over Dealey Plaza. The evil deed had been done, the Professional killer had perfect cover to simply just pack up and quietly slip away from the scene. If it was a Mob-ordered-and-paid-for hit, the assassin would still be paid and the Crime Family responsible wouldn't give a damn who actually fired the fatal shot(s), as long as the Liberal President from Massachusetts was dead. Certainly, the Military-Industrial Complex which Ike had warned JFK about on Inauguration Day for Kennedy, would not be crying crocodile tears over the event. Kennedy had planned on disengaging the Country from the quadmire which Vietnam was rapidly becoming. That would have spelled the loss of Millions, perhaps even Billions of Dollars to the Mighty US Military machine.

One other thing that Matt found very interesting. In the minutes immediately following the shooting, a member of the President's Security Detail recalled having passed a man wearing a suit on the sidewalk underneath the railroad trestle. The man had opened a leather Passport-type case with a badge inside and flashed it to the Secret Service Agent who had merely nodded back to the man. Shortly thereafter, that Agent recalled that he had never before seen the man. That was implausible since all Agents assigned to the President and Vice President were a very tight group and well-known to one another. That seemed very odd. Had someone on the inside of the Security Detail been paid to look the other way or threatened in some way, even though they would have had no knowledge at all of the assassination itself, only that "something would happen in Dallas", a part of which they would not question until it was too late to do anything about it? To Matt, this had all of the marks of the way the Mob did business with those who had failed to cooperate with them. Matt, stopped for a minute and just stood still and shook his head ever so slightly. Yeah, a Mob hit? Yeah, maybe so. That's an interesting thought – now to prove it. Had he done all he could in Dallas. It was time to catch his plane back to LaGuardia.

CHAPTER FOUR

The Cuban Connection

UN Ambassador Adlai Stevenson had recently addressed the United Nations Security Council and had displayed US reconnaissance photos showing completed concrete missile silos, built by the Russians, in Cuba. They were to be filled with Intercontinental Ballistic Missiles, capable of reaching of reaching the entire US mainland and also capable of carrying nuclear warheads. They were irrefutable evidence that such Offensive weapons were being supplied by the Russians to the Cubans. The atmosphere in the entire White House was tense. President

Kennedy ordered US Naval blockade of the Atlantic sea lanes leading to the Island of Cuba. Naval warships intercepted and stopped several Soviet cargo ships with missiles, covered with tarps, clearly visible on the "weather deck" of the Soviet ships. We were literally on the brink of War with the Soviets, who were testing the resolve of the young, new President and his National Security team. Kennedy, from the Oval Office, was in telephone contact with his counterpart in the Soviet Communist Government. The Russian demanded some sort of a quid-pro-quo from Kennedy before he would order the freighters to return to their Russian port. Kennedy badly need to buy some time. What could he offer the Russians for a "deal sweetener". Finally, it was decided that the US would agree to remove some relatively benign missiles from Eastern Europe. The "Cuban Missile Crisis" had ended – it was over. The Media hailed the courage of the President in standing up to the Russian threat. The President had forced the Soviets to back down. In American University academic circles, the President's "victory" had run much more deeply. He had caused the Russians to "lose face" in the Communist World. That feat was deemed to be much more important than simply causing the Soviet ships to stop and return to their port.

Among both the Soviets and Asians, "loss of face" is such a disgrace, that it is often cause for "Summary execution" by the Government. All of this Matt Clemmons knew. His questions and curiosity had to do, not with the Soviets in their interaction(s) with President Kennedy, but rather what he could find out about the reaction by the Cuban President, Fidel Castro. It was Castro's name that had been bandied around as having been behind the killing of Kennedy. The Cubans were not known as being particularly obsessed, or, for that matter, giving a damned about any possible loss of face or prestige in the international community. The Russians were having their own problems with their sagging economy and were increasingly reducing their substantial financial support for their Communist ally in Cuba, without which Castro's Cuba could not long survive. The American Helms-Burton Act had embargoed Cuba from any trade with the US and would continue to do so indefinitely. Castro had been forced to try to curry the favor of possible financial partners in Central and South America. Fortunately for Fidel Castro, the Americans had decided not to try to either resurrect or to enforce the ages-old "Monroe Doctrine" in which President Monroe had tried to warn of "dire consequences" for any Country in Central

America to attempt to threaten America, in any way, to put it overly simplistically. Castro had been free to try to expand his "Cuban Communist Revolution" into Central and South America, through his old friend and surrogate, Ernesto "Che" Guevara. Castro had given Che "Carte Blanche" authority to stir things up to the best of his ability, especially in Latin America, with marginal results, at best.

No, Matt reasoned, Castro had survived the threats of US Presidents going back to Eisenhower. The US Central Intelligence Agency had tried to clandestinely kill Castro, even trying to get Castro to use something straight out of Ian Fleming's James Bond – an exploding pen when he signed some Edict or whatever. Matt reasoned that to Fidel Castro, President Kennedy was a mere nuisance more than a threat that he had to eliminate through such an overt action as underwriting an assassin to do the job. Castro would survive Kennedy, just as he had survived the threats of US Presidents going back to his triumphal entry into Havana atop a tank along with his rather rag-tag group of Revolutionaries who had toppled the US-supported, and corrupt regime of Fulgencio Battista. He, Fidel Castro, had finally rid the Cuban Island of the corruption of the American Mafia which ran the Casinos of

Havana, the prostitution and the drug traffic. And he had been allowed to do it all in full view of, and with the apparent acquiescence of the American Government. No, Matt said to himself, it made no sense for Castro to have either been involved in, or to have financed an Underworld assassination of the young American President. Fidel had had "his plate full" of too many other much more important matters to Cuba than to have had any serious interest in whether Kennedy lived or died. Cuba would go on as Castro directed that it would, as a Communist/Socialist State, no matter who was the American President. It didn't really matter to Fidel Castro one way or the other. The Americans had their problems and he had his. Cuba was a mere unfortunate footnote in American History, to the chagrin of fifty years of American Presidents. It no longer mattered to the Cuban President, one way or the other.

Therefore, Matt summarily dismissed any Cuban "connection" with the killing of Kennedy. There was just, simply no reason to partake in it. Castro would have been quite happy to let others handle the matter which had been nothing more than at most, at one time, long ago, a significant threat to his Island and his total grip upon it, to what it had evolved into – a pesky nuisance. Nothing more – nothing less.

Later in his investigation, Matt would come across something else which would cause him to rethink and reexamine The Cuban Connection. It would resurface, but in another scenario. That scenario, while it may or may not have played any role in the killing of Kennedy, had great significance in its own right. It would directly involve the President, the Vice President, the Secretary of Defense, and most notably, the Secretary of State, Dean Rusk, all gathered together in the Oval Office of the White House on one fateful day, and literally, defining moment in modern American History. The story gets better and more incredible as you read on and as it unwinds. Could this really have happened? Yes, it could, and it did. It's consequences are still being felt and were a defining moment in the US Presidential Election of 2000 when "hanging chads" caused the Florida Electoral vote to be determined by the United States Supreme Court and the the result was that George W. Bush was "determined" (not elected) to be the President of the United States. The Cuban exiles, in Miami, were disheartened by it all.

In some ways, that election can be traced back to that fateful night, in the Oval Office, when Robert Kennedy, then the Attorney General of the US, took the telephone call, on the red phone on the corner of the President's desk, from the Pentagon, which Secretary of State Dean Rusk had actually first answered before Robert Kennedy took the telephone receiver from the Secretary's hands. The caller was the Chairman of the Joint Chiefs. A decision had to be made immediately. SECDEF put an Admiral directly on the line and monitored the conversation. There was a Task Force of the US Navy sitting off the southwestern coast of Cuba. A Rear Admiral was in Charge. He had ordered the launch of US fighter-bomber aircraft from the aircraft carrier which was the flagship of the Battle Group. The fighters were circling the carrier. The Admiral needed the Order from the President to turn those planes toward the Cuban coast to provide air cover for Cuban Nationals who had been recruited by the CIA to invade Cuba and remove Castro and his Communist government. The site of the invasion of Cuba was the "Bay of Pigs". The invasion was taking place as the Secretary of Defense listened-in. The Admiral wanted to personally speak to the President, immediately. Robert Kennedy had the red telephone receiver to his ear and told SECDEF that the President was not immediately available. He was presently conferring with both the Vice President and his National Security Advisor and was not to be disturbed. Bobby Kennedy still had the phone to his ear as he stood alongside the President's desk. Secretary of State Dean Rusk had moved the President's specially designed chair (it had special support for the President's lower back because Kennedy had chronic back pain resulting from his incurable Addison's Disease) back from the President's desk so that the Secretary could lean over the desk with both of his hands open with fingers outstretched on top of the blotter on the desk. Secretary Rusk raised his balding head and looked straight at Bobby, asking, in hushed voice, who was on the phone and what was going on? The President was standing far from his desk in a sort of huddle with Lyndon Johnson and the head of the NSC, totally oblivious to Bobby, who was still holding the receiver of the Red phone. The Admiral was growing more impatient by the second. Dean Rusk stood up and raised his right hand in a gesture for Bobby to hand him the phone. Bobby, with is free hand, waived off Dean Rusk. Then, Bobby told the Admiral that the President was still busy but had decided that the Admiral withdraw all US air support for the invading Cuban Nationals and told Bobby to pass the decision on to the Admiral. Bobby had tried to cup the mouth part of the telephone receiver as he gave that instruction to the Admiral, but Dean Rusk had heard enough to figure out who the caller was. Bobby ended the call with "that is all, Admiral, you've got your Orders". The Secretary of State merely shook his head in both amazement, and total disbelief. Dean Rusk was furious, livid, about what had just happened. Briefly breaking the protocol which applied to everyone in the Oval Office except the President, himself (no first names were to be used, only Official Titles), Dean Rusk 'got up close and personal" with the Attorney General, and said "Bobby, you're the goddamned Attorney General, for crissake. You just made a decision that only the President is authorized to make and that's in the Constitution which apparently you need a refresher course on. In case nobody has reminded you lately, you're the guy who's job is to enforce that Document and not find your own way to subvert it. You really don't get it, do you? Now I'm the guy who has to tell the President of the United States that his brother has just ordered an Admiral of the United States Navy to "recover" all launched US aircraft to the Carrier and cancel all US Air support for those brave souls who will be cut to shreds by Castro's defense forces. Do you fully realize that the CIA recruited and trained those men to do what you just stopped. Now it falls on me to tell the President what has happened. I hope you're happy with what you've done." The Secretary of State silently moved to where the President was standing, muttering, inaudibly, to himself, "son of a bitch thinks he's God". The US aircraft, intended to support the invaders were never launched beyond their holding position directly over their aircraft carrier, to which they returned from their holding pattern. Who gave the actual Order NOT to send the US warplanes ashore to support the Cuban Nationals invading, to take back their homeland from Castro? Now, Matt Clemmons knew. Still, he did not see it as any "deciding reason" for Castro to take any part in the killing of the American President. After all, the invading forces had been repulsed. Those who were not killed outright, were taken prisoner. Castro had personally gone to the site at the Bay of Pigs and had taken full charge of the Cuban defense of his Island. Castro was, and has been a pragmatist. He takes what he can get and merely shruggs off that which he cannot get, as not really necessary anyway to the survival of his Communist State. He is satisfied to rule, with an iron fist, his bastion of Socialism, sitting, as it does, in the warmth of the Caribbean just ninety miles from the United States' Key West. Enthroned and ensconced in Havana, even the US Naval Base on the eastern tip of Cuba does not bother him. Guantanamo Bay was just there, posing no threat to the rest of his Island. "Gitmo" as it is known to the US Navy, is but a sliver of land in far eastern Cuba. Let the Americans play their War Games from there. It causes his Government no expense and poses no threat to the rest of the Island. Fidel Castro probably says to himself, "let a sleeping dog lie"

No, Matt reassured himself, he saws no Cuban connection to the killing of Jack Kennedy. As far as he was concerned, any Cuban Connection was a dead end – it did not exist.

CHAPTER FIVE

Back to New York for
more Investigstion

Matt Clemmons had satisfied himself that neither the Russians nor the Cubans had been involved in any plot to kill President Kennedy. Those two "trails" had come too a dead end. Who might have had any interest in having the President killed? Matt's mind was set on "fast forward", as if trying to eliminate the commercials in a really good television show. In doing so, he asked himself, had he inadvertantly overlooked any key piece of information? He retraced his mental steps and assured himself that he had not. A very big step was to have eliminated both the Russians and the Cubans from his list of possible suspects. He had considered everything and overlooked nothing. He reminded himself that in Security matters, one had to have three key elements – clearance by proper authority, physical access, and a need to know. Absent one of those elements and you did not get access to Classified information. In civilian terms, those elements were, "motive, weapon-causing death, dead body". Known, in the case of President Kennedy, was the weapon which caused the death, and the dead body. Still unknown was the motive. Looking a bit deeper, Matt Clemmons, considered the possibility that there may have been more than one motive involved in the case of Kennedy. In fact, there may have been many motives. The primary motive may have been both "professionalism" and "pay-for-hire" – the "hit man", the guy paid to kill the President – neatly, cleanly – one shot, one bullet, one confirmed kill. The "cloud" hovering over that theory was the gunman Oswald, who had fired three shots, one of which proved fatal..He may have had an "axe to grind", somehow, against the President, but hardly the "stuff" to motivate an assassin. No paid assassin would have fired three shots and then have been stupid enough to have stayed around, especially in a theater, watching a movie. Any paid assassin would have been long gone from the scene and on his way back to wherever. Folks who engage in murder-for-hire, live, for all practical purposes, a normal family life which automatically removes them from the suspicion of both their families and the local authorities. They have "cover" jobs from which they take "leave" of some kind to move onto and complete the next "assignment" and then return to whatever they normally do for an "outward" living. One of them might be your neighbor and you would never know it. It's a cold-hearted and dispassionate business. On occasion, one might even resort to advertising as one such sort did years ago in the San Francisco Chronicle. His ad read, "Have gun – will travel", wire Palladin, San Francisco". It was a television drama with Actor Richard Boone, with his signature handlebar moustache, black western-style hat and six gun, playing the role of Palladin. It was, of course, pure fiction, but it aptly illustrated the point that Matt Clemmons, had considered. Who would ever suspect a paid killer to actually ADVERTISE? Well, none of them ever advertise, per se, yet the best in their "profession" were known by their "clean hits" – "one bullet – one shot – one kill" with not a trace left behind for any investigation. The "machine gunnings" of entire establishments were not meant to necessarily produce a kill – they were only a message that someone "within" had poked his nose in where it did not belong. Message sent – message received – mind your own business, or else. Next time, if there is one, there will be a fleet of vehicles outside, taking bodies to the morgue, capisce? Even the Police didn't dig too far. If it was a Mob-related hit, do a cursory investigation (enough to take any heat off the Major and a Councilman) and send the file to the Archives as "unsolved homocide.".

Matt Clemmons suspected some sort of a conspiracy between the Mafia Families of New York, New Jersey and Miami. The New York Mafia was run by John Gotti, affectionately known as "the Teflon Don" for his uncanny ability to have any wrongdoing just roll off him and onto some hapless underling left to suffer the dire consequences of whatever illegal act may have been perpetrated. No, Matt reasoned, that may have happened, but would have been too obvious, and someone outside of Mob circles would have had to have known. Maybe, just maybe, THAT was the key to it all. Maybe everybody DID know and, for whatever reason(s), just conveniently forgot to tell the Secret Service.

And what if somebody did try to warn the Secret Service? Would those Agents have listened and heeded, or would they have "tossed off" tips as very unlikely scenarios and not worth following-up? Both the FBI (under Director John Edgar Hoover) and the Secret Service had something of a habit of "turning a deaf ear" to information coming from sources other than those unearthed by its own Agents or known, reliable informants. They even looked at information coming from Licensed Private Investigators with more than a slightly "jaundiced eye". Moreover, Hoover's Agents were notorious for their penchant to wade into the crowd gathered at the scene of shots fired with their 38s drawn and badges held high with the other hand, while yelling, "FBI – get back". In some cases, it was a blatant case of the Federal Agents lacking jurisdiction and a simple show of force. None of them ever stood back and watch it all unfold to see who might have benefitted from the distraction/diversion of attention. Matt could recall at least one case he had read about where the shooting "victim" was pronounced dead at the scene by an imposter EMT and a rental van with vinyl signs on its side saying "Coroner". The FBI Agents sent the local Police "packing" while they "secured the site" with much fanfare. Turned out the shooting was fake, using blank bullets. Once inside the van, the "victim" was very much alive and a nearby bank had been robbed, despite a silent alarm having been set off by a teller. The fake shooting had all been just an elaborate diversion from the real crime.

Matt decided to pass his time by a trip to the New York City Public Library where he found and was poring-over a copy of The Warren Report – the final report of the Government's formal Investigation of the Assassination of President John Fitzgerald Kennedy. Heading the Commission had been Earl Warren, former Governor of California and former Justice of the United States Supreme Court.

The new President, who was given the Oath of Office for the Presidency of the United States, aboard Air Force One, still on the ground in Texas, by Federal Court Judge Sara Evans Hughes, had to do his best to get the Assassination behind him and get back to Washington and get about the business of the Presidency and leading the Country. The new President, Lyndon Baines Johnson, faced a formidable task. Yet, he had a unique opportunity to place his own imprint on the Leadership of the Country. Kennedy's Administration had been known as "the New Frontier". Johnson would call his Administration "The Great Society". H would begin by convincing the Congress (of which he had been a part as Senate Majority Leader) to pass his "landmark legislation", the "Civil Rights Act of 1964". It was to be "sweeping legislation" in that it would give "landmark Civil Rights to blacks and other Minorities". In time, it would prove to be the most significant and important Act of the Federal Government since FDRs "New Deal", the Social Security Act, and, arguably the best piece of legislation EVER enacted by the government, the "GI Bill". First, however, the Warren Commission had to undertake and finish its work. Why had Earl Warren been selected to head the Commission? The Commission needed to have the bi-partisan support of the Congress to support and enhance its legitimacy. Earl Warren had been the conservative Governor of California, which is largely why President Dwight Eisenhower had picked him to fill a vacant seat on the Supreme Court. The Senate had confirmed Warren to a seat on the High Court..Then, for reasons known only to Earl Warren, he had turned Liberal and his Court had authored what came to be known as the "Miranda Decision", which gave heretofore, unfathomable legal rights "automatically" to all those accused of criminal acts. It wasn't long before Policemen (and women) all across the Country "knew the drill", as in "you have the right to remain silent. You have the right to an Attorney and to have an Attorney present during all questioning by Police , If you cannot afford an Attorney, one will be appointed by the Court at no cost to you. Anything you do say ,can and will be used against you in a Court of law. Do you understand these rights?" That statement to an accused, recited, verbatim, by Police Officers, at the scene of an arrest, or later, at the Police Station, became a benchmark of American Criminal Law, to the chagrin of many a Criminal District Attorney. Whatever good Earl Warren may have done as the Conservative Governor of the "Golden Bear State", was overshadowed by his Liberal decision of forcing all Police to "Mirandize" all arrestees. Parenthetically, years after leaving the Presidency, Eisenhower granted an interview to some Reporter at his farm at Gettysburg, Pennsylvania. When asked about the biggest mistake he had made as President, Ike replied, unhesitatingly, "He's sitting on the Supreme Court". Nevertheless, Lyndon Johnson chose Earl Warren to Chair the Committee which had the responsibility to investigate and determine who had assassinated JFK. The Commission concluded that Lee Harvey Oswald had been the lone gunman who had fired the three shots which had killed the President and injured Texas Governor John Connally. It also found that Oswald had acted alone, with motive unknown, and had fired from an open window in the Texas School book Depository Building, over looking Dealey Plaza in Dallas, Texas. That, in essence, was the totality of the findings of the Warren Commission. Case closed! At least as far as the new President was concerned, the Case was CLOSED. The Nation had other pressing matters to move onto and Lyndon Johnson was determined to do just that – MOVE ON. Matt had the feeling that LBJ had "stacked the deck", as it were, and had told the former Justice, what he wanted the "illustrious" Commission to conclude, in its findings. President Johnson had his own Agenda, which became known as "The Great Society". He wanted no lingering suspicions from the Warren Commission Report to the Congress, to "muddy the waters" for him. The findings of the Warren Commission wee to be final in its determinations. No stones left unturned, a fanatic had acted alone in his killing of the President. Matt could not find much mention in the Warren Report of the X-rays taken at Parkland Hospital of the President's skull. Only that two bullets had penetrated it. There was no mention of the possibility that someone shooting frontally, from the grassy knoll, might have fired a shot that entered the front of the skull. Had that been been "covered up" in the medical report or had that evidence never been there at all? Matt was satisfied the medical report was accurate, true, and complete. Any possible assassin, positioned on the grassy knoll, had never had the chance to fire a (deadly) shot at the President. There was no more evidence available on the fatal shooting of the President in Dallas, that day.

Matt could not clear his mind of a possible Mob connection to the killing of Kennedy. Absent the Cubans, the Russians, and a chance few shots by an individual unknown to many before that fateful day in Dallas, all else was still unknown. Matt did some further research and found that some weeks prior to Dallas, the President had visited Miami, Florida. The FBI had information that a gunman had been in position to kill the President, but his killing shot had been foiled, at the last second, literally, by someone, attending the passing of the President's motorcade, whose head had prevented a clear shot at the President. The assassin's bullet would easily have passed through that person and still have killed the President, but, to a "hit man", it would have been a "messy" incident. The would-be assassin had "passed-up" the shot, disassembled his weapon, and left the area. To the assassin, there would be more opportunities. There was no reason to maybe leave a trail of evidence. There would be more opportunities as time went on. That event reinforced Matt's thinking that the Mob wanted Kennedy dead. But, whoever wanted Kennedy dead, did they really want to kill the American President, or did they really want to send a deadly message to someone else in Kennedy's Administration, to "stop doing what you are doing" since we have just eliminated your boss and you could be next. All the Government protection will be of no use to you –we will hunt you down, we can and will find you, and we can and will kill you. There will be nowhere you can hide where will not find you. Was that the message that someone intended to send to somebody with the killing of President Kennedy?

Matt could not remove the Mob from his mental list of sources behind the killing of Kennedy. Moreover, Jimmy Hoffa, although in Federal Prison, now, was still a potent force to Organized Labor. He had lots of friends within the Teamsters Union, beholden to him for their jobs in the Union. His influence went far beyond the bars of his cell or the walls of his prison.

He still had access to a telephone and although the FBI may have it wiretapped, he could still speak in "code". Jimmy Hoffa was still a powerful force with both the Teamsters and The Mob. So powerful, in fact, that he could still order a "hit" on his enemies within Labor Unions and they were "carried out" without question. Reliable rumor had it that when Jock Yablonski was elected President of the United Mine Workers of America, Jimmy Hoffa had asked him for a favor. Yablonski had refused. Shortly thereafter, gunmen had entered Yabklonski's house in Pittsburgh in the middle of the night and shot to death him, his wife, and two young children, in bed, as they slept. The gunmen were never caught. A Mob "action" was suspected, but never proven. The Mob's Modus Operandi is to "kill the target and entire family" since, "dead people can't testify against you in Court", nor can they seek revenge.

Fresh out of other leads, Matt turned his attention to the leaders of Organized Crime. Hadn't Joseph Kennedy, the family Patriarch, flirted with the Boston labor "bosses" to float unsecured loans to some unsavory people to get himself elected to President of the Federal Reserve Bank of Boston? He even married Rose Fitzgerald, rumor had it, to "curry the favor" of her father "Honey Fitz", high and influential in political Democratic political circles.

Boston, in the early 1900s had two powerful political groups – both Democrats. One was the Kennedys and the other was the Lodge Family. Neither would relinquish either power or prestige to the other. The Cabot political family was standing in the wings, as it were. The Kennedys were busy currying favor in Boston Social Circles, as a prerequisite to gaining what they really wanted – political power. Becoming concerned about the Kennedys true intentions, the Cabots decided to join forces with the Lodge Family. Boston was a "One Party City" and the Kennedy's had the advantage at the time. Sooo, the "Cabot-Lodge" Family broke off from the Boston Democratic Party and allied itself with the Republican Party. Of the Cabot-Lodge Family, none particularly distinguished him or her self except for Henry, who eventually became US Ambassador to the United Nations, briefly.

A short time later, in Boston, something very curious to Baseball fans occurred. The Owner of the Boston Red Sox was known as something of a philanthropist. One particular evening, he attended an Auction. The details of the Event are a bit fuzzy, but the outcome certainly is not and turned out to be perhaps the biggest even EVER in Major League Baseball History. It had to do with George Herman "Babe" Ruth. What was up for bid at the auction is of no particular consequence. The Owner of the Red Sox bid on it after having consumed more than his share of Champagne. His was the winning bid. He informed the Auctioneer that he wished to be billed for it and that was agreed upon. A month or so later, the bill came due and the Owner of the Red Sox was short of cash. His Accountant told him that he did not have the money to pay for his purchase. The Owner of the Boston Baseball Franchise had to come up with cash and fast. In desperation, he called the owner of the New York Yankees Baseball Franchise. He offered to trade Mr. Ruth for an undisclosed amount of money, but it was enough to cover his purchase from the auction. The Yankees Owner agreed to the price to acquire Mr. Ruth in the trade. That is how "Babe" Ruth became a Yankee. The prestige that "Babe" Ruth brought to the new York Yankees, was all that it took to finance the construction of what is now and what has been Yankee Stadium in the Bronx, New York, and how that Stadium acquired the name "the House that Ruth built" to New Yorkers. It was also the start of what became known, in Professional Baseball circles as "the Curse of the Bambino" Beginning with the signing of George Herman Ruth to a Professional Baseball Contract with the New York Yankees Baseball Club, Inc., they would dominate baseball's American League, to the detriment of the Boston Red Sox, until shortly after the turn of the Century, over fifty years later.

Matt had been mentally recalling that "circumstance", when he shook his head and forced himself back to the task at hand. He was agitated with himself for having so easily become sidetracked, historically interesting, though it was.

Back to the Warren Report. Did it shed any new light on who may have wanted Jack Kennedy dead? As far as he could tell, it did not. However, what the Report did not say and could not say, was what role, if any, Lyndon Johnson may have clandestinely, and surreptitiously have played in the Report's final findings. What instructions, if any, had Johnson secretly given to Earl Warren? Perhaps that no Cuban or Russian involvement or knowledge WILL be found? Kennedy was gone and Lyndon Johnson damned sure wanted nothing found to cause the Nation to "go into either panic or revenge mode" against either Russia or Cuba. He, Johnson, had already witnessed close to that with both the "Cuban Missile Crisis", and the Bay of Pigs fiasco. The very last thing he needed or wanted, was to "saddle" his accidental and fledgling Presidency with National hysteria demanding revenge against an "unknown Entity". If that had been "the bottom line" instruction to Commission Chair Warren, then the Document h eh ad been reading was a mere sham with a foregone conclusion. Like reading a "whodoneit" mystery novel when you already knew "the butler did it". NO, Matt was convinced that there was nothing contained within the Warren Report that could shed any new, or heretofore undisclosed light on The Assassination. There was also the not-so-small consideration that "the Pride of the Secret Service Presidential Detail" was at stake. Those guys do not take lightly to have failed in their ONLY Mission – that of protecting the life of the President, if it means giving up your own. A lot of what they do is extremely Confidential – no, Top Secret. It has to do with which Agents immediately move in, and which deliberately stand back in the event of either one gigantic conspiracy, or a multi-wave assault on the President. Which Agent opens the secret cache of automatic weapons hidden somewhere on the

Presidential vehicle. Which Agents uses his body to literally cover the President. Which Agent takes over in the front seat as "shotgun" with an actual shotgun. Details of that information is NOT what the Secret Service wants described in detail in such as the Warren Report, even though it was Classified by an Act of the Congress for forty years after the actual Event. The Commission's Subject, Mission, Mandate, and actual work will probably never be fully known. The Warren Commission had done its work, completed and reported its findings. Having done that, the Commission "adjourned and disbanded itself".

Matt finally had THAT research behind him. He knew nothing more, really, than he had known before reading THE REPORT. It was time to move onto other sources, information, and possible new leads.

CHAPTER SIX

Exploring the Mafia

Slowly, painfully and excrutiatingly slowly, Matt Clemmons was eliminating the possibilities, at least to his personal satisfaction. He knew how Bobby Kennedy had "taken charge" in the Oval Office during the Bay of Pigs failure. He also knew that since becoming the Attorney General of the US, he had made it his personal ambition to bring the Mafia to its knees. He had targeted the Bonnano, Genovese, and Gamboni Families. Joe Bonnano headed the New York Family, Vito Genovese was in charge in New Jersey, Carmine Gamboni in Miami.

The job of US Attorney General is to determine when Federal Law had been violated. The US Marshall Service is the enforcement arm of the "AG". Federal Marshals are appointed, largely through political connections, or, to put it another way, while they all have merit, they also avoid "rubbing Senators and Representatives the wrong way". They area almost never replaced unless they choose to retire or die in Office. Federal Marshals have lots of Deputies and the Attorney General has Legions of, Deputies, Assistants, and Deputy Assistants. They all carry US Treasury Agent badges and are authorized to carry concealed sidearms if they so desire, since they are all, by virtue of being Licensed Attorneys, also Officers of the (Federal) Courts. The "guidelines" for the Office of Attorney General are specific, but offer great lattitude for interpretation as needed. The Power of a Writ of Search and Seizure is considerable, and usually very specific. however, where more "breadth" is needed as in "somewhere in the house", or "somewhere in the files", the more liberal judges are known to all Lawyers who deliberately seek them out, be it on the tennis court or the golf course. However, leave them alone at a Wedding, Baptism, Confirmation, Bar or Bat Mitzvah.

That's just common sense. As the new Attorney General, Robert F. "Bobby" Kennedy proved to be totally devoid of any such discretion. He and his phalanx of Lawyers would barge right in, "flash tin" (display their Badges), and hand out Search Warrants as if they were coupons for ordering pizza. Not the way to gain the cooperation of anyone from within. More than once, a Search Warrant was literally torn in half and handed back to him with the warning, "so sue me later, but get your slimy ass out of my office now". The typical approach and attitude of Bobby Kennedy was, "We're here, we're legal, we know what we want and we know where to find it, so everybody just clear out and leave us alone to do what we came to do." Needless to say, it was rare when they gained the cooperation of anybody whose property they came to search. Bobby had an uncanny way of irritating people by simply being in the same room.

As Attorney General, Bobby Kennedy took the path of least resistance. He desperately wanted to put the Mafia totally out of business and all of its leaders behind bars in Federal Prison. However, he knew that would take time. He and his team of lawyers would have to tap telephones, gather informants by granting them legal immunity from lesser crimes such as drug trafficking, prostitution, loan sharking, mugging. All of that took time – lots of time – years of time. He figured he had four, maybe eight years to do it all – the term(s) of his brother's Presidency. After that, he would surely be replaced. Bobby knew he did not have that long to do what he wanted to do. He didn't need convictions to do it all, but certainly indictments a the very least. He would have to bring to bear all of his forces and resources toward one, immediate, common goal. Who would it be and how would he do it? He decided to go after the President of the International Brotherhood of Teamsters, Jimmy Hoffa. Hoffa was strong, powerful, greedy, defiant, and easy for the public to dislike with his cocky, outward arrogance. Any charisma with the public did not exist. What a perfect scenario and target for prosecution, Matt thought. It was a classic confrontation. The President of perhaps THE most powerful Labor Union in the World, versus the top Law Enforcement Officer in the free world. A winner on one side would start to fill cells in Federal prisons. A winner on the other side would use his Lawyers to drag litigation through the Federal Courts, appealing one verdict after another, until the term of the President had expired. Bobby Kennedy would the be replaced by a new Attorney General who probably would not wish to pursue the lawsuits which were long in the making with unclear or doubtful outcomes. In all probability, the new "AG" would have no desire to pursue that which would be perceived as the "personal vendettas" of his predecessor. Thus, the Mafia would again escape the long tentacles of its Federal pursuers and prosecutors. Matt thought to himself, the possibilities of this are virtually endless. There is an almost endless number of possible plots and plans for "who loses, who gains, who survives, who doesn't survive, whose power is enhanced and whose is diminished, and at what personal cost? First, however, it would seem to be Bobby Kennedy versus Jimmy Hoffa. Matt told himself, silently, "stay tuned – there is more to come – much more." And then, Matt rolled over in his bed, wrapped his pillow around his head, and fell sound asleep.

CHAPTER SEVEN

Bobby Kennedy versus Jimmy Hoffa – the grand duel

The Protagonist had the power of the entire Department of Justice at his disposal, to use as he wished. The Antagonist had the power of arguably the mightiest Labor Union in the Free World behind him, with all of its ruthless henchmen ready to carry out his orders at his will. One was bound by Federal Law and the Constitution of the United States, and could not exceed the powers contained therein, at least not be caught doing it. The other was constrained by no such boundaries. He could do what he wanted, at will, with no particular fear of being caught doing it, since it would be done by surrogates who would pay the price. They would either willingly serve the jail time for carrying out their orders (usually homicides or arson), or be killed, clandestinely, if they chose to confess rather than go to prison. In the grand scheme of things in life, would Bobby Kennedy dethrone and send Jimmy Hoffa to prison, OR, would Jimmy Hoffa manage to thwart the will of yet another Federal Official? THAT was the question Matt Clemmons had to find the answer to, if he could – if it was possible – if either person had not covered their "tracks" too well to be discovered. Matt was on the trail of two old pros and he knew it all too well. He would keep digging until either he discovered something material to his quest for the truth, or the trail went stone-cold dead.

For the moment, at least, Matt would put his interest in the doings of the Mob on hold. He was much more interested in any possible connection between Jimmy Hoffa's activities and the dogged pursuit of him by Bobby Kennedy's Department of Justice. The US Attorney General seemed both preoccupied with Hoffa and absolutely DETERMINED to put him behind bars in a

Federal Prison. To Matt, it was an abnormal obsession. The Leaders of the Mob Families in New York, New Jersey, and Miami would be a much bigger "prize" for the Federal government to "bag". If your prime interest is to put Organized Crime out-of-business, go after those who absolutely defy you to catch and prosecute them. Don't spend your time with just one person who controls just one area of Organized Labor – transportation – the trucking industry. The Teamsters have no control over rail or air transportation. Probably 25 percent of all US Commerce used rail transport – freight cars. They do all of the really heavy lifting in moving both raw materials and manufactured goods. They move coal, liquids, livestock, and agricultural products (corn and wheat). Had anyone ever known a rail strike that required Federal intervention through the invocation of the Taft-Hartley Act? None that Matt could recall. Why the Federal preoccupation with the Teamsters Union and its President, Jimmy Hoffa. Was there a connection there that Matt had failed to see?

As far as Matt could tell, the Mob ran a relatively "clean" operation, albeit outside of the law. They were into activities which had been going on almost since the founding of the

Republic. Prostitution was perhaps the World's oldest profession. As long as women wanted to "sell their charms" to the public and the public was willing to "pay the asking price", wasn't that, after all, a form of Laissez-faire commerce? The Government will never abolish it, since it meets the basic requirements of "supply and demand" (Economics 101, in College), so why not just try to regulate it and "tax the fool out of it" as has been done with tobacco and liquor? People will always patronize Pawn Shops which are on the "legal side" of Loansharking, just dealing in smaller amounts of "instant cash". Pawn Shops operate within the "usury" laws, while Loansharking does not. Fundamentally, the Mob is just into making large amounts of money without having to work for it and with no W-2 or Form 1099 going to the IRS for purposes of taxation. Whiskey Bootleggers have been doing the same thing for over a Century. The basic difference with the Mob is that those who oppose them are either intimidated into submission, or eliminated. The principle or application of "due process of law" appears, neither in theory, nor in fact, in the lexicon read by the Mafia. Therein lies much of the difference, according to the US Department of Justice.

Matt knew why a lot of Mob "figures" were acquitted when they were "dragged into Court". It had to do with their Lawyers. Government Lawyers generally graduated in the lower part of their Class in Law School. They were happy just to have passed the Bar and become Licensed.. Those Lawyers working for private Law Firms were heavily recruited when they came out of the more prestigious Law Schools, most in the Northeast. Those lawyers could recite Case Law from memory, in Court, in front of a Jury. They were "fast on their feet, glib, and accurate in their recitations". Government lawyers had to ask the Presiding Judge for a recess while they did the Case Law research they did not anticipate having to be able to cite inside the Courtroom. The Government lawyers would still be huddling an a corner of the Courtroom while the lawyer for the accused Mobster would have already posted bail, their client released, and be leaving the Courtroom. The underlying reason was that the Mob always had ready cash to pay for the best Law Schools with a guarantee of well-paid employment upon being admitted to the Bar to practice Law.

The other thing that bothered Matt, was, why was the US Attorney General so interested in prosecuting so many cases which fell within the purview of the Bureau of Narcotics, the Bureau of Alcohol, Tobacco and Firearms, the Department of Immigration and Naturalization? Wasn't that a bit of overkill – a kind of jumping the Chain of command? It seemed to Matt that Bobby Kennedy wanted his fingers in all of the pies of any possible transgression on, or violation of Federal Law.

CHAPTER EIGHT

The Interests of John Edgar Hoover and Lyndon Baines Johnson

It was no secret that both the Director of the FBI and the Vice President had a dislike for President Kennedy. In Director Hoover's case, it was a simple matter of survival as the Bureau's Director. He had kept a secret dossier of political "dirt" on every President going back to Harry Truman, as a form of "job insurance". When Eisenhower was rumored to have been displeased with the Director, Hoover "leaked" the information that Ike, as the Commanding

General in Europe, had had an "affair" with his jeep driver, Kay Summersby. It was intended to cause a marital rift with Mamie Eisenhower. It did not. Mamie Eisenhower just "blew it off". Ike answered, later on by insinuating that Hoover, a lifelong bachelor, had had a longstanding homosexual relationship with his top Aide at the Bureau, Clyde Johnson, also a lifelong bachelor. That was Ike's quid-pro-quo, with the Director.

Some years later, During the Presidency of Richard Nixon, his Vice President was Spiro Agnew, former Governor of Maryland. Well, Agnew got a bit too critical of the FBI at one point in time. Information from Hoover's Office was sent to the Baltimore, Maryland, District Attorney that directly implicated the then Baltimore County Commissioner Agnew in a kick-back scheme with Contractors building the Baltimore Bridge-Tunnel Project. Vice President Spiro Agnew was indicted by a Baltimore County Grand Jury and subsequently resigned the Office of Vice President of the United States. Briefly, the House of Representatives appointed a Congressman from Grand Rapids, Gerald Ford to fill the Vice Presidency. President Nixon resigned from Office from the fall-out of the Watergate bungled burglary of the Democratic National

Committee's Offices. Vice President Gerald Ford ascended to the Presidency and former New York State Governor Nelson Aldrich Rockefeller briefly held the Office of Vice President. It all happened so fast, that most Americans were left sort of "swimmy-headed", including Matt Clemmons. The Order of Ascendancy provided for in and by the Constitution, had worked its marvel. The Republic would continue its sometimes fragile existence and ensure the continuity of the governing body of the Republic, uninterrupted by legal and public mandate. It was well-known that Gerald Ford had never aspired to be President. He was quite happy to stay in the House, representing his Michigan District in Grand Rapids. The Speaker of the House at the time had come to Gerald Ford and told him, "you WILL be Appointed by the Full House, to the Vice Presidency, and you WILL accept the Appointment". And, so Gerald Ford was then the new Vice President. Very shortly thereafter, Richard Nixon was forced to resign the Presidency or face almost certain impeachment for his complicity in what had become known as "Watergate". With Nixon's resignation, Gerald Ford, as directed by the Constitutional delineation of "ascendancy", took the Oath of Office of President. That left the Office of vice President again vacant. Former

New York Governor, Nelson Aldrich Rockefeller was appointed to fill the Office of Vice President. "Rocky" as Rockefeller was familiarly known in political circles, briefly flirted with challenging Gerald Ford for the Republican Nomination for President when Nixon's unexpired ended. It was known that Nelson Rockefeller owned a large horse and cattle ranch in Argentina. No American Authorities had any legal jurisdiction in South America. It would definitely be "problematic" if an unstable government there decided to "mess with" Rocky's Ranch. Even with the attempted resurrection of the old Monroe Doctrine, it would be very difficult to justify "sending the Marines" to defend or "retake" any of Rocky's property that a Coup, upheaval, or insurrection might threaten. Rocky was also on his second marriage to Harriet (Happy) Rockefeller. A heavy portion of the female Electorate had been "disturbed" that Mr. Rockefeller had not fought for custody of a Minor child by his first wife. "Rocky" had also been stung by the loss of his son, Michael, on a sailing expedition in the South Pacific, when the boat apparently capsized in a storm. A song had been written about the incident – it was a folk song whose beginning lyrics were "Michael row the boat ashore, al-le-lu-jah ......" Memory seemed to recall for Matt that the song was recorded by the group, "Peter, Paul, and Mary". Therefore, Rockefeller decided to just finish out the enexpired term of the former Vice President and return to New York to the Westchester County family Estate at Pocantico Hills.

Therefore, Director Hoover, having leaked the information to get Spiro Agnew indicted and forced to resign the Vice Presidency, decided that for the immediate future, at least, all on Capitol Hill were preoccupied with "the new crew at the top settling in". He could well remember, however, when Kennedy was President, being "flat out" told by the Chief Executive to "reign in his forces" a bit or he would suffer the consequences. Matt knew that there was "bad blood" there, between the Director and the President. He had this "nagging" suspicion, which nobody alive could prove, that the Director either knew of, or strongly suspected, a plot afoot to kill the President. He would not act on any information his field forces might come upon in that regard. The Director had, in fact, smugly rocked back in his office chair and reminded himself of the exact words of the President, himself, to the Director, to wit: "reign in his forces ....".

Enter the picture, Lyndon Johnson, the native Texan. There wasn't much "love lost" between him and the President, either. More than once, Johnson had almost drooled at the possibility that he might, someday, become The President. Johnson had enjoyed a remarkable career in the United States Senate (from Texas) and had risen to the very prestigious Post of the Democratic Party's Majority Leader. He had accumulated everything possible to be considered one of the most powerful political figures in the Politics of his time. Yet, however, something was lacking to complete the picture he wanted to leave behind, for posterity. He had not (yet) held the biggest political prize of them all – that of President of the United States, pure and simple.

Matt could well-remember the Democratic National Convention when the Senator from Massachusetts had captured the Convention Delegates to ensure him Nomination for President. Jack Kennedy had kick off his shoes and was sitting on the couch in his Suite, watching the action on the floor of the Convention on the television in the Suite. The time had come for him to choose a running mate for Vice President. Mentally, the young Senator was going down a checklist of the States he would have to carry with the popular vote in order to win the General Election. Texas figured prominently, very prominently, in his calculations. He would somehow have "to carry" Texas. The Senate Majority Leader, from Texas, known to have a Texas-sized ego, would have to have his ego "stroked" to ensure that he would "deliver" the popular vote from Texas to the Party Nominee from Massachusetts. Texas was relatively Conservative territory and Massachusetts was Liberal territory. It would not be an easy "marriage" to arrange. Time was running out for Jack Kennedy to choose a running mate. He decided to send his brother, Bobby Kennedy, to go to Johnson's Suite, a couple of floors higher in the hotel. The "plan" was to offer the Vice Presidency to Lyndon Johnson. They were both certain that the Texan would decline their offer in favor of remaining "the power broker" in the Senate. They wanted only to secure his promise that Texas would vote for the Democratic Nominee. Bobby did his duty at the request of Jack. Bobby was gone for a relatively short time. He came back to his brother's Suite looking thoroughly disgusted. "Well, how'd it go", is he on board to deliver Texas to us?" "Worse, much worse, beyond your worst nightmare, Jack". "What the hell happened, Bob?" "Jack, I made the offer like you told me to. Guess what, the Son-of-a-bitch accepted the offer.

He's now your Vice Presidential Nominee." Jack's response was terse and curt – "SHIT"!

Matt learned that there were rumors that when JFK told director Hoover to "reign in his forces", Hoover was already aware of a plot to kill the President, and that the Mafia was probably behind it. Hoover, knowing that Lyndon Johnson had absolutely no use for any of the Kennedys, should be made aware of just a small part of the FBIs information..Hoover's information made him "pretty sure" that an attempt would be made on the life of the President. Where and where was information that The Director really did not want to know, to ensure "plausible deniability" after-the-fact, if it was to be so. His rationale was that it was hard to look shocked and saddened if you knew it was coming. The less the Vice President knew, the better off he would be.

Thus, Matt reasoned, both Hoover and Johnson had reason(s), "motive" to either want President Kennedy dead, or at least would not "shed crocodile tears" over the finality of the work of an assassin. Neither Hoover nor Johnson wanted their hands soiled in any way in connection with the fate of the President. Whoever wanted the President dead, would have no help, assistance, or information provided by "inside sources", known to either The Director or the Vice President. Lyndon Johnson had his suspicions, but would ask no Federal Investigatory Agencies to do any searching or follow-up. As for John Edgar Hoover, THE Director, his hands were clean. Whatever he knew, might know, or might have been able to figure out, hey, he had been told by THE MAN himself, to "reign in your forces". He had been given a Direct Order, personally, by the President of the United States. That was good enough to "cover the Director's ass".

CHAPTER NINE

Hoffa's name resurfaces

Jimmy Hoffa was serving a life sentence in a Federal Prison for his conviction for Jury tampering. Bobby Kennedy had been responsible for that. Jimmy Hoffa's wife, Josephine was terminally with cancer in a hospital. Her attending Physician got word to Jimmy that his wife did not have long to live. Hoffa asked Prison Officials to let him talk to Attorney General Robert Kennedy. Hoffa pleaded with Kennedy to let him visit his terminally ill wife in her hospital room. Bobby Kennedy summarily refused him his request. Hoffa was close to the point of desperation. What could he, Jimmy Hoffa, offer to Bobby Kennedy to persuade Bobby to let him out of prison just long enough to be at his wife's hospital bedside when she passed away? The AG wasn't interested in listening to anything that Hoffa might have to offer. Jimmy Hoffa had "one last ace up his sleeve" and he played it on the AG. Hoffa told Bobby Kennedy that he knew who had killed his brother in Dallas. He, Hoffa, was willing to trade that information in order to be able to be at his wife's bedside when she died. Robert Kennedy had Jimmy Hoffa exactly where he wanted him, AND, Jimmy Hoffa had no more aces to play in the game. Bobby had the better hand in the cards showing on the table with no more to be drawn from the deck. Hoffa would not disclose what he knew before he saw his wife, and Kennedy would not agree to the visitation until Hoffa revealed his information. It was a classic confrontation and standoff. Which came first, the chicken or the egg? Bobby Kennedy, ever the sly one, loathed by most who encountered him, at best, and thoroughly despised by those who hand encountered his wrath, at worst, kept in contact with Josephine Hoffa's attending physician at the hospital. Kennedy arranged for Hoffa's visit to his wife's bedside, but timed the visit until Bobby knew Hoffa's wife was already deceased.

Kennedy called Hoffa, at the hospital and wanted the information Hoffa had promised to deliver to him. Hoffa told Kennedy on the phone, "screw you, you son-of-a-bitch. You knew she was dead before I ever got to the hospital – now you can kiss my ass." At least that's what Matt learned from those who claimed to have overheard the conversation.

If Hoffa had had the information that Bobby Kennedy wanted to know, his disingenuousness with Hoffa had cost Bobby Kennedy dearly. To put it another way, to the everlasting regret of the Attorney General of the United States, Jimmy Hoffa had had the last word, Whatever information Hoffa knew, Bobby Kennedy would now have to get it from another source. For the first time in his investigation, Matt Clemmons was stymied. He had information coming at him from all directions – all of it seeming to have some validity. And the "compression of time" was almost mind-boggling. Word had gotten out of Bobby Kennedy's telephone conversation with Jimmy Hoffa at the hospital. Bobby Kennedy had just thoroughly "pissed off" his late "hot lead" on who had either ordered, or carried out the killing of his brother. Joe Bonnano and Vita Genovese were left wondering what, if anything factual, Hoffa knew that might be traceable back to them. Joe Bonnano had ordered the "hit" on the President, but only after encouragement from Carmine Gamboni of the Miami Mob Family. Nobody knew who, exactly, either was or should have been the actual "triggerman". Was Oswald the actual assassin or did the hired "hitman" manage to fire the fatal shot first, from the grassy knoll? Or, for that matter, did it really matter at all. The "target" was eliminated and that was the original mission anyway, wasn't it? Bobby Kennedy was on a wild rampage to get the information that Jimmy Hoffa was supposed to deliver to him. Who else could possibly supply that information to the AG, anyway? Did ANYBODY know? And if somebody DID know, unknown to the Mob, who was it, who could it be, or who could it have been? Was there a rogue member of the Mob out there who somehow knew too much? Was there a Capo intent on replacing a Mafia Don? Would Bobby Kennedy, assuming that Hoffa was on the brink of "ratting" on the Mafia, have decided to try to find the answer by putting the squeeze on the New York and New Jersey Mafia? All of Matt's sources had been aware of a "big hit" put out by the mob. They all assumed that the target was Bobby Kennedy for going after the "Syndicate" leaders, Jimmy Hoffa, first and foremost, for their mutual disdain, and personal hatred. The only problem with that theory was that the President was dead and his brother was very much alive, and still on the hunt for the leaders of Organized Crime, Logic did not address that fact. Here was Bobby Kennedy, going after just about everyone who had a Union Card, and, in the process, pissing off all of legitimate Labor groups, as well as those Groups engaged in clandestine illegalities. Yet bobby is still the AG and his brother, Jack, the President, who was enjoying high numbers in the National popularity polls, is dead. To Matt Clemmons, as well as to many others, it just didn't add up – it didn't make any sense. There was a vital piece of the puzzle missing. What was it, or, the better question, who was it?

Well, Matt mused to himself, when all else fails, go back to where the "trail of evidence" was still warm – Jimmy Hoffa. The connection between Hoffa and Bobby Kennedy was obvious. Where was the link from Hoffa to PRESIDENT Kennedy?

Matt finally discovered that Hoffa's appeal to his life conviction had been reduced to "20 years" The Appeals judges had concluded that Jury tampering did not merit the same sentence as

Arson or Murder. "Justice" had been served with a 20-year conviction. A Federal conviction allowed no sentence reduction for "good behavior", or being a "model prisoner". However, Hoffa had been released from prison after serving 20 years. As part of his successful appeal, he had agreed not to run for President of the Union of the International Brotherhood of Teamsters, again. It had been suspected that the new President of the Teamsters, Frank Fitzsimmons, who had gone to great lengths to "clean up" the "image" of the Union after Hoffa's tenure. However, there were still a lot of Union Members around who had remained loyal to Jimmy Hoffa. Fitzsimmons thought that he just might have a problem with the possibility of a "resurgent" Jimmy Hoffa.

Then, something very unusual happened. Jimmy Hoffa, now a free man, was invited to a "meeting" at a restaurant. There was no agenda for the meeting, but Hoffa's adopted son, John O'Brien had invited his step-father, to have lunch with him. They had lunch and chatted about whatever. Then, Jimmy left the restaurant, got into a car, and was never heard from again. Jimmy Hoffa had just disappeared from the face of the earth, never to be seen or heard from again. It was as if he had never existed at all. Nobody knew anything about Hoffa from that time on, or, if they did, they weren't talking. With Hoffa gone, would Bobby Kennedy be content to be rid of him, or would Bobby say to himself, "one down, three to go", as in Joe Bonnano, Vita Genovese, Carmine Gamboni? It was a nagging and lingering concern for the three Crime Family leaders. Could they afford to wait for Bobby Kennedy's next move with his legions of Federal prosecutors? No, their collective thoughts were the Bobby Kennedy's thirst for convictions against the Mob had merely been "whetted" with having jailed Jimmy Hoffa. They figured that they were next on the Attorney General's list of prosecution targets. They could not afford the interruptions to their daily operations, to wait for Bobby Kennedy's next move. On the advice of Carmine Gamboni of the Florida Family, Joe Bonnano of the New York Family had ordered and paid for the "hit" on President Kennedy. Vito Genovese had agreed to the decision.

Still unknown, was the name of the actual "hit man" who was paid to actually firer the shots which were supposed to have killed the President. He was paid for his work even though Lee Oswald may have preempted him by a second or two. Only two people know the answer to that question – one is dead – the other will probably never be known.

The answer to the biggest question in modern American Political History was now very clear to Matt Clemmons. While Americans will debate forever, who actually fired the bullets that killed President John Fitzgerald Kennedy, to Matt Clemmons, the person who decided the fate of the President, the man who may as well have pulled the trigger that fired the fatal shots – the Unwitting Assassin, was the President's own brother, Robert F. Kennedy. He doomed his brother to an assassin's bullet when he jailed Jimmy Hoffa. Hoffa knew who ordered the death of JFK and was going to "rat" on the Mafia. That violated the Mafia Code of Silence. Hoffa had to be eliminated, period. Then there were the "fatal words" of Carmine Gamboni, to wit: "chop off the head of the snake and the tail falls of automatically". JFK was the head of the snake and RFK was the tail of the snake.

Matt discovered one very interesting piece of information, along the way. At the edge of the railroad tracks on the overpass at Dealey Plaza in Dallas, was a large metal box. It was about five feet square and six feet high. It was a storage facility for equipment used to do routine maintenance on rails and crossties. The door to it was secured by a large padlock. The padlock had a serial number stamped into it. The Railroad had a record of all of its padlocks, using that number. In its investigation, the Secret Service checked the number on that padlocked against the records of the Railroad. The numbers did not match. Then, Matt recalled the brief encounter along the sidewalk passing under the railroad trestle of the two Secret Service Agents – the one flashing his badge, and the other who had never seen that Agent before, at the time of the Assassination of the President. Could the unknown Agent have actually been the paid assassin from the grassy knoll, heading away from that metal storage box where he had left his rifle to be retrieved later? Could the lock on the metal shed have been substituted by him for the original one which he had earlier cut off the box? That would explain the difference in the serial numbers on the lock from the number the Railroad's records.

MATT CLEMMONS'
SURPRISING DISCOVERY

Matt had his strongest suspicions of his investigation. Eliminate the Cubans and the Russians and what's left? Every time he discounted a possible connection, the only culprit left was the Mob – the Mafia. He made one last trip to the New York Public Library and found a surprising discovery. Yes, the Congress had "Classified" the Warren Report for Forty Years, after-the-fact. And yes, that Report was now de-Classified. But there were no surprises to be found there. President Lyndon Johnson had give the Commission its "marching orders", to start with the premise that the Assassin WAS Lee Harvey Oswald, and work back to findings that supported that conclusion. However, Matt also found a transcript of a tape of an FBI wiretap on the phone of the New York Mafia Don to the Head of the Miami Mafia. For no apparent reason, the two Mafia kingpins saw no reason to be very cryptic about what they said and discussed. It was all remarkably "open conversation. Essentially, it went something like this. "Eh, Paisano, you learn any more Spanish since lat time? Fuck you, you ignorant bastard, and I'm not any Paisono – I'm a respectable Miami businessman, capisce? Oh are we sensitive today? Sorry, I didn't mean to step on your short, limp dick. Hey, I get more ass than a toilet seat, so fuck you. Now, what the fuck do you want from me? I need your permission to put out a hit on somebody. Must be somebody big for you to ask me for an okay. Who the hell do you want taken care of? It's Bobby Kennedy, the President's brother and Attorney General. He wasn't satisfied jailing Jimmy Hoffa and the rumor from the Federal Courthouse is that he's asking a Federal Judge to approve a gob of search warrants to look into my files. I don't need that shit. It will put a stop to all my street operations until his kid lawyers are finished crawling up my asshole and looking around. The numbers games, the rackets, loan sharking, drugs, prostitution, you name it, will all have to shut down till he's finished looking. Then the cheap street thugs will move in and start stealing from my runners and bag ladies. I can't have that. I want to put out a Contract on that rat-bastard Attorney-General Bobby Kennedy. Are you with me nor not? No, I am not with you. Leave the prick Attorney-General alone and take out his brother, the President, instead. You forget our Sicilian expression, "kill the head of the snake and the tail automatically falls off". Chop off the head of the snake, Jack Kennedy. For THAT, I will give my permission. What's the Contract worth, anyway? Fifty Grand. Okay, count me in for ten Grand of that. That rat-bastard Bobby has caused me huge losses from rum and European booze I can't get out of Cuba anymore. I had a deal going with that Commie Fidel to bring it to Miami in small, unmarked planes flying below coastal radar at just 100 feet off the water 'till that rat-bastard Bobby started bribing the night shrimpers to watch for them and gave them fucking radios to alert the fucking Coast Guard. Same thing with my drug runners from South America. Fuck that mutha fucker, just fuck him, but don't ice HIS slimy ass, ice his brother, instead. Remember, the head of the snake ....?" Okay, I will honor your wishes, my friend, but you may have to send some Enforcers up here if the street thugs who got no respect for their elders start stealing from my people. I will do whatever I can to assist my brother in New York. By the way, you got any idea who tried to ice the President when he visited Miami a while back? This is my turf, for Chrissake, NOBODY takes a Contract in my town without me knowing about it and approving it. Word on the street is that whoever it was is a fucking ghost. Covered his tracks real good. Had a clear shot at the President until some lady spectator's head got in the way. Musta been a pro who wanted a real clean shot. In my fucking area some hotshot tries to whack the President and none of my people have a clue. That's just not right. It's not according to our Code of Ethics. It's bullshit – that's what it is, just plain bullshit. Gotta go now, you got my blessings to take out the President, but not Bobby. I'm outta here."

EPILOGUE

The Murder of JFK

Matthew Clemmons had completed his "investigation", unofficial, though it was. Nobody had come up with a plausible rebuttal. Sooo, his conclusion was every bit as good as anybody elses.

The Emil Zapruder film had been timely and interesting, but inconclusive. Nobody had an explanation for the different serial numbers on the lock securing the metal storage box along the railroad tracks. Nobody had either identified or remembered the face of the "Agent" who had flashed his badge to other Agents under the railroad trestle.

In all of the confusion at Parkland Hospital in the Emergency Room, nobody recalled exactly how many X-rays were taken of the President's head. Three cranial X-rays had been taken of the President's head – all from the rear. All showed "entry" bullet wounds and one exit wound at the front of the cranium. The bullet exiting from the front of the skull had never been found, or, if found (it HAD to be somewhere in the Presidential Limo), it's existence had never been reported and was NOT in the Warren Report. The three bullets allegedly fired by Lee Oswald had presumably lodged somewhere in the President's upper body or head. It had been the decision of the Medical Examiner, and, concurrently of the Forensic Pathologist, not to desecrate the President's body further to recover the deadly pieces of lead. For those who watch such as "CSI-Miami", it is easy to question why such as matching bullet striations to weapons would not disclose an "alien" bullet not fired from Lee Oswald's rifle. However, the year was 1963 and the only "computer" at the time was either an abacus or a mathematicians/ engineers sliderule. A sense of both History and "perspective" must be applied. One ER Nurse at Parkland had been given an X-ray photo by a

Secret Service Agent and told that the machine had not been calibrated properly and the image was too blurred to "read". She was told to take it directly to the hospital incinerator and be sure that it burned completely. Had the X-ray POSSIBLY contained a clear image of an entry wound from the FRONT of the President's skull, which would have subsequently complicated the findings of the Warren Report and caused unnecessary problems for the new President Johnson?

Given what Matt had learned about the Mob and the hit-men they hire, those guys don't rest until they finish the assignment. It's more than a matter of ego – it's a matter of "professional pride". The rifle contains one bullet only. One slow and steady trigger-squeeze – one shot fired – one kill – definite and deadly. Automatic weapons, spraying bullets randomly were used to send a message. The "pros" are not into that shit. Whoever "whacked" the President in Dallas was probably the same one who passed up his chance in Miami. Had he gotten off one shot from the front, from the "grassy knoll" within a milli-second of Oswald's three shots from the Third Floor? Had the President's head become "sandwiched" between two Assassins? Oswald walked to a theater, bought a ticket and took a seat to watch a movie. Mr. "X", walked to the metal shed next to the railroad tracks, placed his rifle inside (he'd already cut-off the lock with the Serial Number on record at the Railroad), and left it in place, so that it would appear to be fully intact and locked unless closely inspected or pulled-upon. He replaced it with a similar-looking lock and firmly secured the replacement lock. He was probably the same man who flashed a fake FBI Badge to the passing Secret Service Agent walking underneath the railroad bridge. He then blended-in with the normal pedestrians of everyday Dallas. He may even have gone to Jack Ruby's Nightclub for a beer or whatever. Jack Ruby may even have known him and his "assignment". Ruby may have shot Lee Oswald in revenge for screwing up the planned "hit", and messing up an otherwise "clean Operation". For all anyone knew, Jack Ruby could have been the local coordinator as a "sleeper Agent" for either Castro or Khrushchev. Castro and Khrushchev both had MOTIVE – Khrushchev for Kennedy's Naval missile blockade of Cuba, and Castro for the failed delivery of the missiles. All of that was plausible, possible, and most certainly INTRIGUING, yes. However, during that time, Castro had his own serious Domestic problems with an almost non-existent economy. Khrushchev had his own Domestic problems with a rebellious Politburo and an ambitious Leonid Breshnev wanting to become General Secretary of the Soviet Communist/Socialist Party. I was all POSSIBLE to Matt, but too much of the stuff of a "far-out" piece of fiction for him to believe. "Yeah, it's there – nah, not much credibility."

Sifting back through hundreds of pages of notes, Matt decided, in his own mind, the ONE incident that had cast the fate of President John Fitzgerald Kennedy. It was when Jimmy Hoffa's wife, Josephine, lay on her deathbed, in a hospital, from cancer when he was in prison on a Federal charge of Jury Tampering on a Racketeering charge. He had phoned Attorney General Bobby Kennedy, asking to be released just long enough to be at his wife's bedside when she passed away. Bobby Kennedy had phoned the hospital and had spoken to her Doctor, asking for his best guess as to how long she had to live. Given that information, the AG authorized the release of her husband, to arrive at the hospital about an hour later than the Doctor's guess. Hoffa had told the AG that he knew who ordered the hit on his brother and who carried out the hit. When Hoffa arrived at the hospital and his wife had already passed-on, he called Bobby Kennedy and told him, "you son-of-a-bitch, you KNEW and delayed my release just long enough. Now, fuck you, you slimy Irish rat-bastard." Shortly thereafter, Jimmy Hoffa was to meet his step-son, Charles "Chuck" O'Brien, at an Italian Restaurant, in the parking lot. It was a "we need to talk" kind of meeting. Jimmy Hoffa got into the back of the other car and has never been heard from since. Among some, thought to be "in the know", it is believed that Hoffa, as "pissed off" as he was at Bobby Kennedy for denying him the right to be at his wife's bedside when she died, he was still willing to tell the AG who killed his brother in return for the AG lifting the ban on Hoffa ever running again for President of the Teamsters Union. Trading that information was almost irrelevant to the Teamsters top bosses. What WAS important, was that Teamsters President, Frank Fitzsimmons, had turned the Teamsters into a legitimate Trade Union which had "cleaned up its act". Threats and intimidation were a thing of the past. No longer was anyone using the lucrative Teamsters' Pension Fund to underwrite illicit activities or for "front money" for drugs and racketeering. Fitzsimmons feared that if Jimmy Hoffa ran for Union president again, and somehow won, corruption would again return to the Teamsters. Therefore, it had been arranged to "make Jimmy Hoffa disappear" FOREVER.

At the time of President Kennedy's death, the law provided that ANY body, whatsoever, was the "property" of the County Sheriff and Coroner of that particular County in whatever State. When President Kennedy was killed, there was a considerable brou-ha-ha among local Officials as to who had actual, legal custody of the President's body. FBI and Secret Service claimed priority and ultimate jurisdiction. Dallas County's Sheriff and Medical Examiner refused to release the body to ANY other authority, Federal or otherwise. Ultimately, reportedly, it all came down to a "show of force" outside the Emergency Room at Parkland Memorial Hospital in Dallas. There were simply more Federal Agents (some with weapons drawn) than local Police or Sheriff's Deputies. The President's body was taken by the Secret Service to Love Field and placed aboard Air Force One in the Cargo Hold for the trip to Andrews Air Force Base in Washington. Jackie Kennedy rode, with her husband's body, along with the newly-sworn-in President Lyndon Johnson and Lady Bird Johnson, for the flight to Washington. Since that time, the Congress has acted and passed a Law that applies ONLY to the President of the United States. Paraphrased, it states, In the event of the death of the President of the United States, while in Office, outside of the District of

Columbia, the body shall rest in the sole custody of the Senior Agent-in-Charge, Federal Bureau of Investigation, Department of Presidential (Secret Service) Security and Protection.

www.ingramcontent.com/pod-product-compliance
Lightning Source LLC
Chambersburg PA
CBHW031855170626
46807CB00004B/1737